∙≠▷ **D A Y A N** ◁≠∙

White Eurocka
Akiko Ikeda

English translation by
Michiko Tomomi

DARK HORSE BOOKS®
Milwaukie

As soon as winter came, a horrible cold wave came through the area of Tachiel. There was usually no heavy snowfall at this time of year, just snow flurries, dancing in the air.

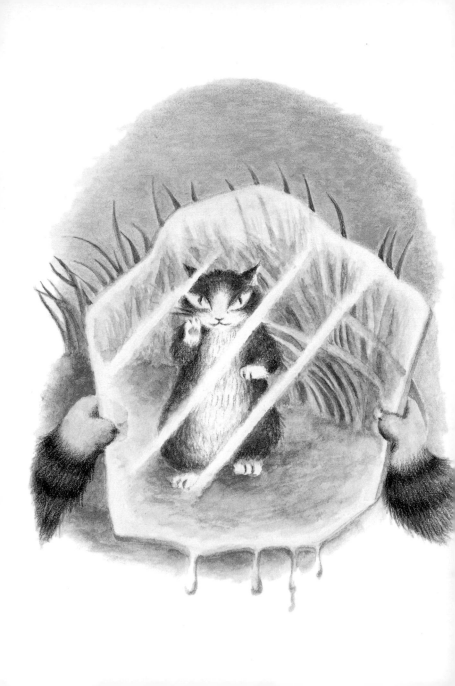

But the north wind raged with such might that nobody was able to go out of the house. As the Eurocka Festival approached, the north wind finally lost its power, but the cold did not let up.

Dayan, who got tired of staying indoors, went out to Daz Pond to play. He would break the thin ice layers at the water's edge with a stone or look into the ice and pretend it was a mirror.

"Oh, there comes Jitan!"

"Shall we go to the beach, Dayan?"

"Well, yeah . . ."

Dayan actually didn't want to go to the beach on such a cold day, but it had been a long time since he last met Jitan. He was just simply happy that Jitan invited him to go along.

As they came close to the beach, they heard many loud voices, as if there was a sports event going on.

"Wow! What's going on?" The beach was completely filled with many unusual animals they had never seen before.

As Dayan and Jitan approached them, Mister Slick, who was looking from the window of his hut, came out to greet them.

"What is this all about?" he asked harshly, as if Jitan had created the situation. Surely, Jitan would know the reason for this, otherwise, why would he think of going to the beach?

Jitan, instead of answering the question, spoke to a particularly big and ugly animal.

"Is this year, THE year?"

"Yeah," the walrus answered, in a voice that echoed. "I felt the wind said so."

"We felt so, too," agreed the seals.

"I sensed it from the wind, with my whiskers."

Several penguins on a large iceberg merrily chorused, "The north wind carried us here, house and all."

"The animals of North are probably the ones who will come for this year's Eurocka Festival. I thought so since it's been so cold with the north wind blowing, and now I figure my guess could be right. See, there are so many animals here to welcome them." As Jitan said this, Mister Slick shook his head in disbelief.

"We still have five more days before Eurocka. Are they going to stay on my beach till then?" Mister Slick, who loved being alone, didn't like the commotion.

Having heard about the animals, the inhabitants of Tachiel started coming to the beach, one by one. Some came with sample dishes of festive foods for Eurocka and some came in the hope of becoming acquainted with unfamiliar animals. As they became friendly with each other, some invited the animals to stay overnight in their homes.

Dayan, who was also full of curiosity, asked a couple of polar bears to come and stay at his home. He had grown used to large animals by this time.

The fluffy fur of the polar bears felt so nice.

In the end, the penguins alone remained at the beach of the Aral Sea, and dove off the icebergs and caught fish. Their time spent here was just as pleasant as it was at North.

By then, Mister Slick enjoyed looking at them from the window of his hut, more than anything else. He even wished he had more time before Eurocka came.

During the late afternoon of
Eurocka, the guests from North
and the inhabitants of Tachiel
climbed Mount Tachiel together.
The penguins swam up the
Torol River, and with the help
of the animals, finally arrived
at the top of the mountain.

Then, at the moment Jitan's bow
fell upon the strings of his violin,
the opening dance awakened
the Snow God, announcing
the beginning of the festival.

As their dancing shook the earth, snow began
to fall. It turned out to be the heaviest

snowfall they had ever seen and the guests
from North were more than happy.

The heavy snowstorm aroused the old magic, and the door of Eurocka started to appear at the top of the white fir tree. Then, from the opened door, a particularly large lump of snow, in the shape of a ball, flew out, spun as it fell, and got buried in the snow.

What first appeared was a jet-black nose. Then, this lump shook off the snow and opened a pair of deep black eyes.

The dancers surrounding the dazed
polar bear cub began dancing again.
There had never been such a big

crowd before, during Eurocka.
Nor will there be in the future.

When the dancing ended, the white guests from the white land disappeared into the eternal white snow.

Dayan's Collection Books
Vol. 3: White Eurocka by Akiko Ikeda.
Copyright © 1993, 2008 by Akiko Ikeda. All rights reserved. Original
Japanese edition published by Holp Shuppan Ltd. The United States
edition published by Dark Horse Books.

This United States edition is published by arrangement with Wachifield
Licensing, Inc. through SUN R&P CO., LTD. in Japan.

Publisher Mike Richardson
Editor Robert Simpson
Designer Tina Alessi
Art Director Lia Ribacchi

English translation by Michiko Tomomi
Cover painting by Akiko Ikeda

Published by Dark Horse Books
A division of Dark Horse Comics, Inc.
10956 SE Main Street
Milwaukie, OR 97222

darkhorse.com

First Dark Horse Books Edition: March 2008
ISBN 978-1-59582-127-0
Printed in China
10 9 8 7 6 5 4 3 2 1